MW01088499

THE DIVINE FARCE

Also by the author

The Love Song of Monkey
(Leapfrog Press)

The Intelligent Movement Machine
(Oxford University Press)

THE DIVINE
FARCE

MICHAEL S. A. GRAZIANO

A LeapLit Book
Leapfrog Literature
Leapfrog Press
Teaticket, Massachusetts

A LeapLit Book
Leapfrog Literature

Published in 2009 in the United States by
Leapfrog Press LLC
PO Box 2110
Teaticket, MA 02536
www.leapfrogpress.com

Distributed in the United States by
Consortium Book Sales and Distribution
St. Paul, Minnesota 55114
www.cbsd.com

Cover Painting: panel from *The Last Judgment*
c.1445-50 (oil on panel)
Rogier van der Weyden (1399-1464)

First Edition

Library of Congress Cataloging-in-Publication Data

Graziano, Michael S. A., 1967-
The divine farce / Michael S.A. Graziano.
p. cm.
ISBN 978-1-935248-04-0
1. Humanity–Fiction. 2. Self-actualization (Psychology)
–Fiction. 3. Forgiveness–Fiction. 4. Optimism–Fiction. 5.
Psychological fiction. I. Title.

PS3607.R39935D58 2009
813'.6–dc22
2009030901

Printed in the United States of America

For Florence B

CHAPTER 1

We were in darkness. It was our home. The vertical, cylindrical hollow was about two feet in diameter—tight for three adults, just large enough for us to breathe up against each other or to shuffle slowly in a bumping, awkward revolution.

The curved inside surface of the wall had a nubbled texture against my fingertips like painted concrete. The slick feeling reminded me of a water-resistant finish, perhaps a high-gloss bathroom sealant or a hard resin. I couldn't scratch it. I couldn't see the floor in the dark, and I didn't have the maneuvering space to bend down and touch it with my hands, but I prodded it with my toes and decided that it was probably a grid of metal bars welded together. The grid spaces were not quite large enough for a toe to get stuck.

The flat ceiling, a few inches above my head, was made of the same nubbly solid material as the walls. It was punctured with perfectly round holes like bullet holes, each about the width of a finger. I stuck my index finger up into a hole as far as I could, but all I felt was a narrow shaft. Air and fluid bubbled continuously out of the holes and made a mumbling garble of sound that filled up the space around us. Without the air trickling in we would have asphyxiated. Without the liquid dribbling on our hair and running down the sides of the tube, we would have dehydrated.

At first I thought the liquid was blood. *They*, whoever *they* were who had put us in here, had a refined enough sense of malice to feed us blood. It was warm but not hot, viscous but not oily, and I imagined that it had a salty and sweet smell, although I had trouble distinguishing the odor of one thing from another in that cramped space. Maybe the salt smell came out of our own naked and perspiring bodies.

Thankfully, the fluid turned out not to

be so horribly arterial. When I put aside my dread, I was able to identify the stuff. It was, of all bizarre things, pear nectar, and had the slightly grainy texture of pureed pear. It was ambrosia, of a sort. It was food and drink and dermal moisturizer in one. As soon as I realized the identity of the liquid, the smell of pear became overwhelming. In time I adapted and couldn't smell it anymore.

Arguably we should have been grateful for the nectar, but it didn't succeed in mollifying us. We stamped, we shouted, we pounded on the walls. Of course we did. We felt sick with panic. We shook with rage. We sobbed. But none of it helped. If I hit the wall, slamming it with the soft part of my palm, lunging at it with my shoulder, I accomplished nothing more than a wet slapping sound, a dull ache, and a bruise that I could feel afterward for a while. None of us could hear any indication of a hollow space behind the wall. Its solidity was so absolute that I lost the ability to imagine emptiness outside our microcosm. In my mind the universe was filled up infinitely with concrete, and at its center was one tiny bubble in which our randomly assorted souls had been entombed.

I wanted to jump up and land hard on the metal floor, to dent it with my heels if I could—but my head cracked into the ceiling, and when I landed, the floor was so slippery with pear nectar that my feet went out from under me. I flailed, bashing against concrete and flesh, and my two prison-mates shoved me back onto my feet again. None too gently. Our tempers were brittle.

Rose was the only one of us who could manage to sit down. She had a more delicate build and could fold herself into the slippery space between our bodies. She felt over the metal grid of the floor and reported that there were no bolts, no screws, nothing that could be unfastened. Everything was welded solidly. We asked her to grasp the lattice and give it a hard shake, but she said no, she couldn't, the spaces between the bars were too narrow for her fingers. She bent down her head until I felt her cheek bumping my foot, and then she hollered, her voice resonating down through the pipes, but we never heard any sound back.

Why? *Why* are we here? she muttered as we helped her to stand up again. Surely the most fundamental of questions. Why are we here? What should we do? It is what it is.

Our voices were so resonant in our sarcophagus, whispering and vibrating around and through my head, that all our sentences felt to me as though they came from my own mouth. I had trouble distinguishing. I would think, Did I say that? Did I just mutter something out loud, something unpremeditated that came out in a falsetto? Why would I do that? Am I insane already? No no, it's just Rose. She spoke, not me.

I thought of her as Rose because that was the color of her voice. In absolute darkness, lacking any stray photon of actual color, my brain was beginning to invent it. The sound of *his* voice was hemlock green, and I thought of him as Hemlock or Henry or Mr. Henry Greene. The sound of my own voice was blue. Brother Brian Blue, with a monkish connotation in my mind. She had a warmth and clarity to her voice, he had an acerbic edge, and I had a reflective depth. Our shades changed depending on the mood, from pale, pastel, delicate, thoughtful, to the fiery brightness of emotional revelation, to the nearly black hue of teeth-gritting rage. We all three traveled across a vast space of emotion. We couldn't help it. We were so squeezed side-to-side that our souls squirted out promiscuously over the emotional landscape.

Even beyond the mixing palette of our voices, we were immersed in sonic color—the bubbling constant background yellow of pear juice, the iron-gray bumping of our feet on the metal floor, the silver-white squeak of a hand or shoulder rubbing against the moist wall, the smoky sawing of our breathing, every sound amplified by resonance, the strobe constantly changing but also never-ending. It had a numbing quality.

It is what it is. Hemlock was a philosopher. Sometimes his commentary was bitter and succinct, and sometimes he opened up with enthusiasm. He seemed to go through cycles, like the rest of us. Better just take it for what it is. That was his most bitter refrain, and it ran through all our minds. Why are we here? What can we do? It is what it is.

We had no mutual barriers. At first we might have resented physical intrusion, but let a week pass, let a year pass, let moments trickle into moments until the concept of the temporal increment is entirely lost—and psychological barriers dissolve in the lukewarm pear nectar. Taboos fall and liberties become ordinary. Touch replaces vision. We understood each other through touch. The pads of my fingers knew their bodies, at least the upper halves that I could reach as I contorted my arms in the narrow space, my elbows clunking against the walls. He was half a head shorter than me and more thickly built, his hair missing in a circle on top, his cheekbones wide and sturdy, his lips thin, his smile clever, his nose squat, his chest strongly muscled and slightly barreled. He

smiled more than Rose or me, but the smile
often had a quality of self-directed cruelty,
his lips stretched thinly over his teeth, the
blades of his teeth exposed. He had a hobby
of sarcasm.

Rose was the smallest and most physically
delicate of us. The top of her head came
to my chin. She had long hair, heavy with
fruit moisture. Sometimes she pushed it out
of her face and tucked it behind her ears.
She had a thin, oval face and a small mouth
that, in its most relaxed state, opened into
an equilateral triangle, the lower lip forming the base of the triangle, the upper lip
forming the peak. That delicate peaked
mouth gave the impression, grievously
misleading, of girlish naiveté. Her skinny
arms were strong, the cords of her muscles
standing out when she exerted herself. Her
shoulders and collarbone were so thin that
they reminded me of the folded wings of a
bat, and her breasts were like a stingy after-
thought of padding on an otherwise unpad-
ded frame. She had an energy to her movements and voice, an enthusiasm that could

not be entirely squeezed out of her and that sometimes turned to a quick anger.

I was an upended mop. Ropey wet hair on top of a long thin body. Imagine a plastic bag of cleaning rags tied to the middle of the mop handle and dangling down. That was my gut. A steady diet of pear nectar did not help my physique.

I wanted to sit down. My feet hurt, my heels ached, the muscles of my thighs burned, and yet there was no sitting down. No lying down. No kneeling. No squatting. Hardly slumping. I slept on my feet. I licked the wall and drank nectar on my feet. I urinated on my feet. I passed a thin gruel of defecation while standing on my feet. I stood on one foot and then the other to give them each a few moments of rest. I sighed. I wept. Sometimes I beat the wall with my fists and shouted obscenities so lurid that Rose and Hemlock would snigger, or touch my back with nervous fingers to calm me down. I beat the side of my head against the wall. Sometimes I did truly want to hurt myself. The sage became savage. My legs trembled from the pain in my knees. But the world is what it is. You get used to it, as you get used to anything. I became like some stiff-legged species of ungulate that stands every waking and sleeping moment of its life. The only release from standing that I could ever hope to achieve would be to die, rot, and let my bones fall in a heap on the grid floor.

Don't worry, Rose called up to us as she was sitting on the floor. You're not missing much. If I could stretch out my legs, that would be something else. A wistful hue tinted her voice. But no. I'm pretty much jack-knifed down here. The only benefit I get from sitting down is feeling out your toes and assholes.

Despite her instinct for diplomacy, Rose had the most grotesque sense of humor of the three of us. She had a laugh that came from the belly and sounded like a dying cow.

Under the circumstances, sex came naturally. It was an inevitable consequence of imprisonment. It was a rule-based dance. We did it to pass the time. We're tinker toys, Henry said, displaying his talent for sardonic wit. We fit together every which way. We never developed jealousies—we didn't have enough psychological space between us for jealousy. At the root of jealousy is a fear of abandonment, and we had no possibility of abandonment in that place. If Henry and Rose were at it together and I was busy turned the other way licking juice from the wall, I didn't mind. It didn't even occur to me to mind. We often did it all three together. Sex helped us to achieve a single warm blend. It was emotional nectar and we maintained ourselves on a regular diet of it.

But sex was not our obsession. If we were not sleeping, or drinking juice, or cursing, or bruising ourselves against the wall, or silently plying our own personal tics, then mainly we argued. Talking is what kept us sane, if that is what we were. We had long, elaborate conversations with cosmologically immense pauses between phrases and thoughts. Sometimes I lost track of what was actually said and what was a thread of thought in my own mind, so that the conversations wandered into the eccentric and irrational.

For a long time, I wondered if we were in heaven. An institutional heaven, with limited resources, that had slotted us into the only available accommodation. I imagined that the universal block of concrete was honeycombed with compartments, billions for the ten billion people who had ever lived and died, each stall crammed to capacity with one or two or three souls. A brilliant organizational trick, it was applied game theory. A person alone—hell. No matter how deeply reflective, no matter how self sufficient— eternal solitude—hell. Two people—as good as hell. Three people, a triangulated complexity, strife and forgiveness, alliance and conflict, a polyphonic piece of music sometimes dreadful in its dissonance, sometimes uplifting in its harmony—heaven. My optimistic theory was that any three people, crammed together for a long enough time, would eventually find a mutual harmony. The rules of heaven were minimalist. They were elegant.

THE DIVINE FARCE

If I was right, then we would remain here for eternity, our guts engulfing each other like amoebas, our breaths in each other's faces, our feet turning into waffles against the metal grid of the floor, our voices resonating through each other's skulls. Paradoxically, that thought of eternity took away some of my fear. To be trapped for a day, even one day, was brutal. A year was sickening. Any finite amount of time implied an eventual release, and my longing for release hurt me in the gut like chronic appendicitis. But eternity—that was on a different level of conception. It forced the mind to acquiesce entirely and accept the here, the now, and the comfort, such as it was.

Those are the thoughts I had when I was in a forgiving mood. I forgave them for their flaws, Rose and Greene. I forgive you, I said to them in my mind. I forgive you. And I felt better.

We settled into our own bizarre hobbies to fill up the time.

Henry Greene's hobby was his constant exercise. He did quarter squats—he couldn't squat down any farther in the confined space—and he jogged in place and he did what he called resistance training, pressing his palms against the opposite sides of our tube and tensing every muscle in his torso. His exercise had a frenetic quality, as if he were trying to distract himself from the fundamental truths. For all his sarcasm and his disparagement and his cruel smile and his burly posturing, he was fragile. I could sense it as if my nerves had grown directly into his skin. Sometimes he would fly into insanity. He'd shriek with a strangled, pear-gargling sound. He'd thump his head against the wall—and if anyone had the physical strength to knock out his brains it was our Henry. The cracking sound of skull on cement was sickening. We'd grab him and Rose would wrap her thin strong tentacle arms around his head. He'd fight us, screaming and staggering, and we all three would get our share of bruises. He was much stronger than me. After a while he'd stop surging under us and calm down. Or give up.

Well, he'd say after a long pause, in resignation and also in apology, it is what it is.

My own hobby was even more bizarre. I licked the painted concrete. I had gone past the nectar and become a connoisseur of the wall itself, learning the pattern of bumps in the slightly uneven surface. The tongue is a sensitive finger, and every bit of wall that I could reach became familiar. We turned about, we shuffled positions. Sometimes I was standing near one part of the wall, where the nubs and indentations made a lopsided spider, and sometimes I was near another part where the pattern resembled a ship with wind-blown sails. I came to know hundreds of private constellations. Animals, buildings, words, faces—it was my obsession. The ability to lose myself in a vast mural of the imagination, and in that way to separate myself occasionally from the others, was necessary to my equilibrium.

Don't get too fat and crowd us out, Henry said. To them I was merely snarfing liquid off the walls, and I heard them snickering behind me conspiratorially. I ignored them.

I kept my back to them and my tongue to the wall, until Rose beat on me with her open palms, laughing, and said, Sage, turn around, we love you.

They called me Sage because I rarely talked, and when I did, my phrases came out as *non sequiturs* like bizarre Confucian sayings.

Rose would twist herself down between us in angular spasms until she was sitting on the floor, one hand cupped gently around my ankle, the other hand around Henry's ankle. In this way she held us together, as if she were a telegraph, as if she felt the need to physically hold us in order to transmit her thoughts to us. She would hum, her head resting against my thigh or his. That was her hobby and her obsession. She did not have a particularly beautiful voice, but the resonance of our shower stall made up for a great deal. The music wandered. She had a knack for improvisation and let the melody tunnel its way here and there. As she hummed, her music worked into my brain and turned into a metaphor. Our world was made of intricate, interlocking strands of music—anger and resentment, despair, loyalty, trust, humor, contempt, forgiveness, alliances switching and switching, Rose, Henry, Brian, primary colors, however harsh, however outrageous, as long as the parts fit together into the workings of a larger whole. A tessellation, a giant unity.

Love.

Then again, sometimes my soaring philosophy meant nothing to me, and I thought, like Hemlock, it is what it is. It isn't heaven, it isn't hell, it's simply where we are, and it stinks. It stinks literally. It stinks and it hurts. And the people here are driving me crazy.

The hardest part of the wall is through, I blurted out.

The what?

Say it again?

What does he want?

Is he sleep-talking?

I held their hands and led their fingertips to a sandy spot on the wall about an inch across. Tiny granules came away with each touch. The sealant that coated the wall had worn through, and the underlying concrete was now exposed.

Chapter 2

The divine intelligence, if there was one, had a cruel sense of humor, waiting patiently until we had lost any concept of freedom, until we had become connoisseurs of our prison, until we had gone beyond resignation and had achieved wholesale emotional dependence on each other and on the feel of each other's bodies, until we had turned our predicament into a philosophy and a cosmology, until we didn't know anymore whether we wanted to stay or leave. Then it gave us a weakness in the wall.

The sandy spot repelled and attracted us. We were afraid of it. Touching it, however gently, could only exacerbate the blemish by rubbing off a few more grains. But at the same time, we wanted to prove to our senses the incredible—the wall was vulnerable. If one of us tried to prod the spot in secret to satisfy a private urge, the touch made a rather obvious grainy sound like a black and white flicker and blew the secret. Then we would shout at each other to leave it alone, to stay away from that part of the wall.

Rose and Henry accused me of wearing out the spot by obsessively mapping my private constellations on the surface of the wall. Henry lost his mind, screaming at me until he worked himself into a shaking panic. We thought he might try to hurt himself. When he had shouted himself through to the other side of his rage and was safely calm again, Rose took a turn castigating me. I listened earnestly. I did take their rage seriously. But finally I lost patience with their complaints and pointed out the absurdity of the accusation. You can't wear a hole in concrete with your tongue, no matter how many decades you work at it. The truth was simple: the wall was vulnerable to erosion. Sooner or later, the entire surface was going to wear away around us. We were evidently not in eternal stasis.

THE DIVINE FARCE

We argued about what to do. Should we face the inevitable, get it over with, rub a hole straight through the wall and see what was on the outside? That suggestion hopped from one to the other of us. Sometimes it seemed right and sometimes it seemed too dangerous. Even if the death of our microcosm was inevitable, why hurry it?

The argument came down to the obvious question: what, exactly, is outside the wall?

Molten lava, Henry Greene said with absolute conviction in his voice. You poke a hole in that wall, and we fry. He didn't subscribe to a literal interpretation. Sometimes he told us it was boiling water, sometimes a trillion centipedes. His fears seemed to be an expression of conservatism. He was afraid of losing the familiar.

More wall, Rose said. You can tunnel through that stuff for a thousand parsecs and it's all solid concrete.

More stalls, I said. Just like ours.

As soon as we had articulated our opposing cosmologies, the outcome was foregone. We had to find out who was right. Even

Henry had a paradoxical glee in his voice when he said, You'll see, you'll be sorry.

We stopped avoiding the sandy spot and took turns scratching at it. The bare concrete soaked up moisture and turned soft, came apart bit by bit, trickled down the wall in a grainy mud that got under our feet and scratched against the metal grid. I didn't know whether our progress was fast or slow. We had been in constant circumstances so long that any change at all seemed fast; but rubbing a hole in concrete with our fingers was a decidedly inefficient process. When I scraped at the wall a bit, stopped to rest my hands, slept for a while, woke up, drank some nectar and took another turn at the wall, I could hardly feel a difference since the last attempt.

When the hole was a few inches wide and deep enough to put my fist in, it seemed like an obscene thing, like a tumor in reverse. Touching it made me feel ill. We had ruined our world.

Don't worry, we'll make ourselves a little extra space, that's all, Rose said. Her vision was the most comforting. We could hollow out an entire castle for ourselves, given sufficient time. Living room, complete with table and chairs, bedroom, exercise room, bowling alley, gallery of sculptures on pedestals, steps up and steps down to halls and chambers, kitchen with pear nectar oozing from the ceiling, as long as the thin trickle of sand from our excavations didn't clog the drain. Maybe we were *meant* to take our comfort into our own hands and create a fabulous mansion. The world is not what it is: the world is what you make it.

Until the centipedes, Hemlock said grimly, twisting his hand in the hole, working as hard as any of us.

My own vision was the most disturbing. Death by centipede or by boiling water was nothing compared to the dread of finding new people. In my cosmology, sooner or later, maybe in ten feet, maybe in a thousand, we'd crack into someone else's microcosm. I didn't know if we had the emotional and psychological space between us to adopt any new people, and I didn't know if those people would appreciate our company.

I had a sudden image of us as nucleons in an atom. We were meant to be together. We were bound in a stable group of three. The laws of nuclear physics held us in an eternal exchange of ideas. If I was right, then we were about to perform an experiment in atomic fusion, crashing into another atom with possibly catastrophic realignment of the nucleons. I might lose Rose or Henry to some new attachment, or I might be snared by another alliance myself.

Despite all our anxieties, we were seduced by that hole in the wall. We wore it deeper because we wanted to know.

And we were all three wrong.

I was scratching at the back of the hole, now about six inches deep, when my finger poked through the concrete into an empty space. My first instinct was to freeze. The other two waited silently, guessing from my reaction that something new had happened.

I didn't feel any boiling water, or lava, or centipedes gnawing on my finger. I didn't feel anything soft like human flesh, or wet like nectar, and therefore I didn't think I had poked into somebody else's microcosmic stall. I drew my finger out and light spilled back out of the hole.

Light.

After eons of darkness.

An ectoplasm, an infection of the brain almost like pain, almost like joy. I wanted it to stop. I tried to stuff my finger back into the hole, but shaky with panic, I knocked out a bit more concrete, and my finger wasn't big enough anymore to plug the leak. I spread my hands over the hole, and the stuff seeped out anyway. We all three hollered and clutched our eyes, turned away, huddled the best we could on the far side of the stall, cringed against each other, and I could hear Hemlock moaning, Didn't I tell you? Oh, didn't I tell you this would happen?

We weren't burnt up. Hemlock was wrong. Nothing untoward happened to us. After a while we took our hands off our faces, opened our eyes, turned around, and realized that we could see. We could see each other. Hearts beating hard, we could see the inside of our world.

A ghostly shaft of light poked in at us and dispersed around our home like a thin gas. The walls were painted institutional aqua marine, slimed and stained and gummed with pear, dingy and ordinary, looming close around us. The contrast between what I saw and what I had imagined in my mind was grotesque and difficult for me to understand.

The people beside me were unfamiliar. A small woman had scraggly hair and a fungus-white face. Her shoulders were skinny and her hips were gigantic. All her stuffing seemed to have slid down into the lower half of her body. The short balding man had a deeply lined face, dark beady eyes that glared around him here and there, and stringy muscles that twitched on his arms and chest and in his cheeks. My own body was alien. It was a rubber suit, saggy, yellowed, and dripping with pear slime. It didn't belong to me.

The woman smiled nervously, exposing

small separated teeth, and whispered, "Is it for real?" I closed my eyes and her voice turned rose again. Is this what we are?

We began to scratch our way out of the chrysalis. We couldn't stay inside any longer, now that we *saw*. Vision had trivialized our tiny world. We used to be three parts to one soul, locked in introspection, and now we were three separate people who hardly knew each other—if we were people at all. Three troglodytes. Three grotesques. Three grubs in a pupa. Three fools in a concrete pipe. I could conjure back my old companions by closing my eyes, but they were ghosts in my mind. The light was like the final, crucial pinch of ingredient in an alchemy experiment gone wrong—it had condensed us from fluid concepts into flawed, dried crystals of reality.

I think the woman with the scraggly hair found some twisted humor in the situation. She bared her teeth. The short man was angry. For myself, underneath a layer of confusion, a layer of dismay, nostalgia for the long gestation that was irretrievably over,

I could not help a touch of exaltation. I didn't know what that light meant, where it came from or what was outside our stall, but I felt expectant.

When the hole was large enough to see through, we took turns peering out, but for all that we peered and stared and argued over what we saw, we couldn't make out any more than a dirty gray cave too gloomy to guess its size.

The concrete must have gradually taken on water and lost its strength. Henry kicked hard at the wall in a spasm of fury, his teeth gritted and the lines of his face falling harshly around his mouth, and a chunk of cement fell out. A few more kicks and bashes and we were free.

CHAPTER 3

I could lie down. It was all I wanted. I lay on my back with my arms and legs spread out. My organs felt shifted, rearranged by gravity, and the sensation was strange and opulent. The floor of the cave was pebbly and uneven, stained, steaming, blotched with pools of muck and tangles of loose hair, but it was smooth enough for me to lie on.

Presumably I still reeked of pear—it was soaked into my pores—but I couldn't smell it anymore. The stifling, moist, fruity, fecal, urea smell of our tomb was gone, or at least greatly reduced. The air was a warmish body temperature much the same as before, but the sweeter smell and the constant gentle movement of wind through the cave gave me the sensation of freedom.

The walls rose up fifty feet to the ceiling,

an exhilarating generosity of space. My soul expanded beyond the limits of my ugly rubbery body to reach up into that emptiness.

The hole that we had knocked in the wall was more than twelve feet above us. I could hardly see it in the dim light. It looked like a fold or crack in the uneven cave wall, merely a shadow. A few bits of broken concrete lay around me. My hands and knees were scraped and bloody from the fall, and I could still feel the pain of the impact as if my bones had a memory. Even if I had wanted to return to our old home, it was unlikely now, because we had no obvious way to climb back up. I didn't mind. I wanted to lie where I was, spread out to occupy as much space as I could, my eyes open, my eyeballs roving and taking in the luxuriant expanse of the new world.

The walls were artfully sculpted and stained to imitate natural, water-carved limestone. They were black, lumpy, and dripping with stalactites. The sculpting was excellent and I would have been convinced by the imitation, except that I had just come from inside the wall and knew it was concrete. I wondered how many other unhatched people were sealed in the wall, trapped in painted cells, lost in universes of thought. I looked around carefully and saw shadows, cracks, folds everywhere up to the ceiling, but I did not know if they were the remnants of pods long since broken open or simply a part of the uneven faux façade.

The cave itself was gigantic, football fields across. The light filtered down from what appeared to be dim bulbs scattered across the high ceiling, but the bulbs were so weak, and the light was so reduced by the time it reached the floor, that anything more than a few yards away faded into a guess. A dense shadow occupied the far end of the cave. I didn't know if it was an entrance to another chamber, or merely a place where the light bulbs had burnt out.

We were not the only people in the cave.

I lifted up my head and stared around the chamber. Here and there people sat in isolation. The ones near us were hunched, their heads lowered, their arms wrapped around their knees or their stomachs, their hair long and greasy, falling around their shoulders and spreading over their backs like shawls, pale angular fragments of body peeking through the weave of the shawls. They looked starved and catatonic. One woman looked at us blankly and then her eyeballs rolled slowly to another spot in the cave. Her expression never changed. The sight of three people bursting out of the wall and falling at her feet apparently hadn't affected her. Farther away the people were harder to distinguish in the gloom, and in the distance they looked like boulders dotting the cave floor. A thousand people must have been in that cave, but the space was so large that it gave the impression of a sparse and lonely population condemned to semidarkness.

Whoever these people were, whatever they had passed through to get here, they evidently didn't appreciate the resources given to them. To live in a room so expansive, and huddle on the floor taking up as little space as possible, to have absolute freedom of movement and not move, made no sense to me. Something was wrong with them.

The closest man was sitting just beside me, hunched and torpid like all the others. He was a thickset balding man and I realized suddenly that I was looking at Henry. Henry Hemlock Greene. My companion, sunk in the dismal mood of the rest of the room. I sat up and stared at him. He was cross-legged on the rocky floor, his fists loosely curled in his lap, an incredible dismay in the lines of his face. He had a bleeding bruise on the side of his forehead that he must have gotten in the fall, but I didn't think he was sad about the bruise.

When he saw me looking at him he smiled grimly and said, "It's all over," his voice thin and unrecognizable without the usual resonance.

Rose and I crowded on either side of him.

"What's over?" she said, wrapping an arm around his shoulder. "Don't be silly. We're all here."

"Sure," he said. But he couldn't get the hopelessness out of his face.

I felt an enormous love for them both, even though they were no longer what they used to be. Rose's song was gone, her warmth was gone, the feel of her body was gone. Only her triangle mouth remained recognizable, like a caricature of herself. She sat patting and soothing a sad little man with a bruise on his bald head. Unprepossessing, naked, flabby, dirty, wet people no better or worse than I was, they had only the faintest hint of familiarity about them. But that hint was enough. It was all we had. It bound us together against the strange and unaccountable. I needed their familiarity wrapped around me for protection and therefore I sat in a warm huddle, feeling quite paradoxically irritated and impatient to explore.

"I want to try the far end of the cave," I said. "I think there's an exit."

We stood up, three in a row, arm in arm, and set off across the cavern.

I was used to standing on thin round

bars. Here, the sharp debris of pebbles hurt the soles of my feet. The act of walking also puzzled me. I hadn't done it for eons. You fall forward, catch yourself with your foot, then fall forward again, then catch yourself with the other foot. Who invented the process? It's a bizarre jerky shuffle. We staggered across the cave floor, our feet sometimes splashing into muck, sometimes slapping onto rock, the grime and hair catching around our toes and ankles until we had trailers dragging behind us. A few of the people that hunkered around the cave looked up at us, but nobody seemed to care. A few heads turned, a few glassy eyes flickered our way. All the sad faces in the room could not stop my excitement. Whatever was wrong with these people, I did not have it. At any rate, I wanted to explore the new world before I decided on a state of personal gloom.

The shadow at the end of the cave was an unlighted tunnel cut into the wall, arching up just above our heads. The three of us held hands and stepped carefully into the darkness, feeling our way with our toes.

After a few bends in the passageway, we reached a second lighted cavern, this one filled with a greater stir of people. It had the same lofty ceiling sprinkled with round, dimly lit circles like shrunken moons. Steam rose up from the floor and swirled near the ceiling in the light of those moons. All around the cavern at the base of the walls entrances gaped, some of them dark cracks in the stone, some of them lopsided arches. People filtered in and filtered out, wandering across the open space between, cringing, muttering, hurrying as if they had a definite goal in mind, or drifting as if the concept of goal had permanently left their heads. They showed no interest in each other or in us.

We stood in the middle of the crowd, holding hands and staring, egregiously out of place as if camaraderie were a *faux pas* in this gloomy country. But if it was, nobody bothered to correct us. Nobody cared. People flowed around us as if we were nothing, as if we were piles of rock in the center of the cave.

THE DIVINE FARCE

They were all naked except for their feet. At first I thought that everyone wore black shoes and socks, but it was only dried muck. Looking down, I noticed that we already had on the same shoes, although we didn't yet have the socks.

If there is a part of the brain meant to comprehend other people, to look and judge and intuit the motives behind the faces, to sort the sheer diversity of appearances, that brain part must have lost its work ethic in the easy years of an elegant three-way interaction in the dark. Now it was overwhelmed. I could not absorb what I saw. At a distance the people were shadows and as they moved closer they loomed into focus, as though I were looking at details of an old faded painting through a magnifying glass. Ancient paunchy jiggling faces, mouths partly open in the concentrated effort of breathing, lined faces, veiny noses grown into the knobs and blobs and beaks of decrepitude, crumpled lips, hair scraggling and twisting down over foreheads, eyes peering out behind strings of hair, pupils

MICHAEL S. A. GRAZIANO

skittering suspiciously, broken teeth, enormous teeth that stuck out at wrong angles, neat small teeth like knick-knacks packed into a suitcase, thin faces like blades carved out of bone, skin so starved and transparent that it revealed the blue veins kinking under the surface, faces as black as the artificially painted walls of the cave, as white as the circles of moon lighting above, as purple as a new bruise, and yellow as an old one, young faces with wide eyes, toothy grimaces of effort, scowls of anxiety, giant nostrils like scale models of the cavern itself, thin nostrils like scalpel cuts, chicken necks pleated and sagging and bouncing with each step, sack torsos, stick torsos, wire torsos bent up and bent over as if osteoporosis had turned the human body into a flexible toy, sunken abdomens exactly as though an autopsy had removed the organs and stitched the skin back over an empty hollow, rolls of abdominal fat that ballooned down to the thighs, breasts like boxers' fists, like dollops of grease, like cheese, like twin fish hanging down and slapping against the belly, penises

44

that wagged and slapped and bobbled, that
stuck out like a monkey's thumb, that hung
like a dog's tongue, like an octopus tentacle
draped possessively over two sea urchins,
dirty curls of pubic hair stiff with dried mu-
cus, loose gaping vaginal lips, pursed and
crimped lips, labia that smacked open and
closed in the rhythm of running, genitalia
lost in fat, genitalia huge and glaring like an
open sore on a gaunt pelvis, bloated bodies
on skinny legs, elephantine legs rolling with
excess skin, scarred lumps for knees, hairy
kneecaps, muck slathered to the hips, to the
shoulders, to the top of the head, buttocks
like external hearts pumping and squeezing
with each step, like party balloons filled up
with grease and sewage, strings of hair hanging down from assholes, stringy muscles on
thighs, fat lumps of hands swinging beside
hips, fists clenched, hands open, fingers
hanging like long killed snakes, delicate
hands and powerful meaty hands, hands
clawed in rage, chicken-foot hands, eagle-
claw hands, giant feet like camels' hooves
that slapped the ground and splashed the

sewage, small thin long-toed feet like a
monkey's feet, monkeys—literal monkeys—
hairy little gray gaunt dog-like four-footed-
handed monkeys scrambling over the floor
with terrified upward glances and squeaks,
ostriches rushing past, feathers fluffed out
in startle, great muscled necks and reduced
heads swaying loftily above the crowd,
pterodactyls, their wings ripped and shat-
tered, hobbling on their claws, their pointy
heads turning anxiously this way and that,
alpacas with great sad eyes, horseshoe crabs
clacking on the stones, giant sloths, potbel-
lied pigs, fruit bats, gnats, a rhinoceros, or
it might have been a gargantuan hairy ar-
madillo, a small theropod, that is to say, a
two-footed, tropical-colored red and blue
and yellow and green carnivorous dinosaur
about the height of my shoulder—but mostly people. I could not shake the feeling that
the animals were people in unusual circumstances. At any rate, nothing tried to eat us.
No creature paid attention to any other.

Caught in the flow of bodies, we staggered through an archway into the noise

and stench of the next cavern where the crowd was even more dense and the floor was slathered ankle deep in sewage. Creatures barked and screamed and clawed as they wedged their way through the crush. We had no control over our movements and my hand was wrenched out of Henry's grip. He stared at me in terror, the dim light glinting from his eyeballs and the slightly irregular bald top of his head, as he and Rose were driven by the currents one direction and I was pushed in the opposite direction. They were still together, struggling to get back to me, and then the gloom turned them into shadows in the distance and I was alone in the crowd.

CHAPTER 4

After the slow ages of nothing, I craved a hideous din. I wanted to take in the world chopped up into sensory fragments and sprayed into my brain through the eyes, ears, and nose. My mind was reeling and for the moment I loved the vertigo and forgot who I was. I thought Henry and Rose would be easy to find whenever I was exhausted by the new experiences and needed a rest—but I didn't yet understand the scale of the place.

I let the crowd jostle me until I fetched up against the cave wall and was herded through a crack into the next room. Then into the next. Some rooms were so dense that they spewed people, and some were less crowded and were like vacuums that sucked in the mob. The décor was repetitive. Each cavern had a tall flat ceiling littered with

dim lights, black walls festooned with stalactites, a carpet of muck and broken stone
under foot, and dark exits branching all
directions in exponential confusion. The
labyrinth was immense.

I was used to standing calmly without end
and had good strength in my legs, but here
I was constantly moving, knocked off balance by the hustle of other bodies, hit in
the eyes by visual jumble, and occasionally
bowled over by passing rhinoceroses. Something immense stepped on my foot with a
two-toed hoof, and in the mud and filth I
couldn't see if I was bleeding. I stubbed my
toes and cut my feet on stones buried in the
muck. Flies landed on the corners of my
mouth to drink my spit. I tried to fight my
way through the crowd, but the effort was
too much. I let myself drift with the flow,
but the drift never ended and never gave
me any rest. A trillion centipedes, Henry
had said. Boiling water. Molten lava. He was
more right than any of us.

I drifted, starved and dizzy, my energy col-
lapsing, my stomach, used to the constant

lubrication of pear nectar, now an empty sack, the inner sides rubbing against each other painfully. I croaked out the names, "Henry, Rose!" but nobody answered. Faces loomed past me but I never saw the same face twice. The crowd seemed limitless, the labyrinth endless, and I began to perceive that I had lost my friends and had very little chance of finding them again.

Eventually I stumbled into a cave that was less crowded than the others. It had only one entrance and therefore the traffic did not flow through it. My ears felt numb in the sudden quiet. The cavern was dotted with torpid people squatting as if they were tombstones in a disorganized graveyard. They must have crawled out of the rabble and given up the fight. Sad, beaten, worn-out people with nothing left but this: they had found a quiet place to sit on the floor and give up.

At first I thought I had found our starting cave. I was suddenly eager. If I could find the starting cave then the labyrinth was not so large after all. But when I stared around the cavern, I realized it was not the same. It was too small. The labyrinth must have been replete with dead-end chambers, some larger, some smaller, holding the derelicts and failures.

I wandered among the human tombs. When I found an open place on the floor, I sank down, cradled my cut-up feet in my hands, and let my eyes drift weakly around the cavern. I had become one of the derelicts. No no, I told myself. I'm different. I'm not as bad as that. I'm going to rest for a moment and get up again.

And go where?

I didn't know the answer to that question.

I picked up a loose fragment of rock to scrape the shit from my legs. While I was scraping I tried to plan what to do next, but I couldn't concentrate while my guts hurt.

"Where do I get some food here?" I said out loud, to nobody. Nobody answered. The people sitting near me did not even stir. My voice had no blue tint left. It had no richness, no thought, no reflection. It was a thin, characterless voice, merely a sound. I had lost not only Rose and Henry but myself too. The space around me was so large and vacant and unresponsive, so little of myself came resonating back at me, that I didn't know who I was anymore beyond an eye that saw and a skin that felt and a stomach that was empty.

In a rage I picked up my bit of rock and threw it at the nearest person sitting in a heap of knees and elbows. The stone whacked him on the ribs with a hollow sound and clattered on the floor. He cringed, gave out a little cry, and turned to look at me over his shoulder. He was a tiny man. His face was ancient and ugly, his eyes wide, his loose skin pouched and pulled back from his nose, his hair sticking out around his head in gray wisps.

"Where do I get FOOD here?" I shouted at him.

He stared at me and didn't answer. Finally he turned away and hid his face.

I hated myself for being cruel. I was alone, hungry, and cruel. And I missed my friends.

The moment that finger of light had poked into our world, I had lost my connection to them. Now they must be in the same state that I was—starved and in dismay. I hoped they were still together. I couldn't stand the thought of them alone.

I grabbed my hair—the pear nectar that had soaked into it had dried and stiffened and made good handles for my fingers—and I rocked and moaned and snapped my head back and forth and ground my teeth. None of it helped, of course. Theatrics don't work if nobody cares. Writhing is never a useful balm to the soul. Eventually I sat still, hunched, worn out, my hands in my lap, waiting to die and desiccate into a mummy. I had never felt so empty, both gastrically and emotionally. I had helped to knock a hole in heaven. I had walked away from it much too eagerly, and now I felt more sad for it than for me. I felt sad it was over, as if our triangulated love was a thing with a soul, and now it was dead, and only the valueless components were left, hopelessly scattered.

THE DIVINE FARCE

I didn't have the energy to get up and search for my friends. Not yet, I told myself, holding onto my empty stomach. Later. After a rest. But I was lying to myself. I didn't want to face a search through an infinite crowd. What was the use? What was the use of staggering through a mob of people, staring at each face I passed, when a thousand other people flickered by me in the shadows, and a million other caves had yet to be searched, and nobody stayed in one place? What was the use when I was starving and could hardly stand up? Maybe, if I sat absolutely still, they would come and find me. Maybe.

It must take a long time to turn into a mummy. I sat and waited, but didn't seem to die. Maybe my pear-fed belly sustained me. Maybe death was impossible in this place. The light never changed. The dim orbs on the ceiling never went out. Sometimes the people sitting near me moved a limb, scratched a leg, resettled, coughed. Occasionally a new person wandered into the cavern and sat down. All around me I could hear the quiet breathing of hundreds of dismal people.

I let myself wallow.

Rose, singing Rose, where are you? Where is your gruesome sense of humor? Where is that warm and nectar-wet hand that you used to curl around my ankle? Henry? My Henry Hemlock Greene? Where is your pestiferous sarcasm and your quarter-squats and your lectures on exercise? Where is your emotional fragility that we tried to protect? Why did I want to leave a world of minimalist perfection, to explore something unknown?

What can I do?

It is what it is.

I watched myself getting thinner. The sack of my belly shriveled. My hands shrank into claws. Since the light never changed, I had no way to measure time.

Sometimes I was visited by the hallucination that the pain in my gut was no longer inside me, but was really a little brown and gray monkey sitting next to me on the cave floor, sneering at me. The monkey would grow more and more solid until it looked about to stand up on all fours and scamper away, taking my vitality with it. That vision always startled me, and when I blinked, the monkey would disappear and the pain would migrate back inside my gut again.

"You," I called out to the man I had hit with the rock. "I'm sorry. I don't know what I was thinking."

The little old man didn't respond. I thought he might be dead already, hunched over, facing away from me. No, when I watched him closely, I could see his back moving slightly as he breathed. I wondered if I should throw another rock at him to get his attention, so that I could apologize.

But I didn't have the energy to find a rock or throw it.

My awareness was disintegrating.

Then in the detritus of my mind I hit on a thought that was quite pragmatic. It must have been forming for a while, building up like an earthy residue on the inside of my skull as the rest of my thoughts dried up.

Since the floor was covered in sewage,

and sewage was the end stage of digestion, a supply of food must therefore exist somewhere in this place.

The thought helped to focus me. It had no bitterness or self pity about it, no drama, no wallowing. It also had no high-flown philosophy. I was not a sage anymore. I was no longer the deep thinker of a group of three. I was alone, I was a nothing, I was a stomach. If I had nothing to do, and nothing to care about, and no hope, and no reason to think, and no friends, at least I could get up off my emaciated and begrimed backside and look for food. It was better than doing nothing.

So I stood up, trembling on skinny legs, my hands and knees enormous, my gut mostly empty skin, and took a few steps among the crowd of breathing skeletons. I felt a certain disquieting fellowship with them from long proximity, but I said to them, Not yet. My voice came out in a scratchy whisper. I'm not yet ready to give up, you guys. They ignored me.

Chapter 5

I had lost all sense of wonder at the gumbo of bodies in the caverns and instead was focused on a goal. Every creature here, human or animal, must crave food. Logically, therefore, I should look for the densest part of the crowd. Instead of trying to escape the insanity and find a place to rest, I pushed into the thickest mobs I could find. I was persistent. I got into caverns so crowded that we were skin to skin, squeezed so hard that breathing was difficult. I stood patiently for hours in the crush, then took three steps, then was forced to stop again. If I saw the crowd flowing out of an archway like a viscous substance under pressure, I made my way toward that arch and worked my way in.

The densest cavern that I found must have had ten thousand people fighting, clawing at each other to open up a way for themselves, climbing onto each other's backs, crawling through the underworld of legs, shouting, boiling across the floor toward the far wall. I saw goats scrambling with their sharp hooves on top of the crowd, treading over the mosaic of heads, shrieking horribly and sinking back out of sight. I saw mountain lions leaping from head to head, their claws digging into people's scalps. I saw the tall neck of the Loch Ness monster sticking out of the crowd, leaning anxiously toward the far wall, but even the monster couldn't make any good headway. Somebody grabbed my hair and tried to pull me back—my eyes watered from the pain—but I wrenched my head free and surged forward. I did not give up. I put all my energy into wedging my gaunt body into the cracks in the crowd. Bit by bit I came closer to the goal, and the goal was food.

I could smell it first, a dry, spicy, dusty smell. Then I was close enough to see the metal food trough. It was made of old sturdy blackened iron and ran the length of one wall. It stood about waist high. Those at the front of the crowd fell into it, or were pushed into it by the pressure of the mob behind them, and then scrambled around inside shoving something into their mouths. They were frantic to get down as much as possible. Bits of food spilled back out of their mouths as they slammed more in. The crowd nearby reached into the trough to drag people out and make room for more, so that eating was a race with time. The people that were tossed out, their mouths crammed with extra food, crawled away and trickled out of the cavern through side exits.

When I reached the trough, I was hit from behind and knocked head first into the food. I panicked because I didn't know if I would drown in the stuff, but it turned out not to be a sludge. The trough was half filled with thousands of little brown hard biscuits, each one like a coin about an inch across. They were continuously replenished, tumbling out of vending holes in the wall, raining down, clanging and thudding into the belly of the trough, adding to the ear-numbing din of the room. I knelt, dug my fingers through the biscuit disks and let them sift back down onto my knees. I heaped them around my naked body. I banked them up onto my chest. The smell and the slightly oily, grainy feel of the food was bliss. I put a biscuit in my mouth and found it so hard that I had to crack it in my back teeth. It had a bland, cardboard taste, but felt gratifying as it went into my stomach. I began to cram in as many as I could, chewing frenetically, wincing as slightly too large or too sharp pieces slid down inside my throat and scratched my membranes. I didn't have time for caution.

The trough seethed with creatures stumbling against me and crashing on top. The largest species had the luxury of residence—nothing was going to pull them out. I did see a young tiger pulled out by its tail. People kneeling in the trough snarled and bit to fend off the hands reaching in at them. In a glimpse I saw a man on his hands and knees, his mouth to the bottom of the trough, sucking up loose biscuit dust. In another glimpse I saw a woman twisting biscuits into her rectum, presumably as a capacious storage for later. Her mouth was already stretched so full that her face looked cancerous.

As I clutched a biscuit close to my face, working hard to chew down the current mouthful before jamming in the next one, I was startled to see a pattern stamped into the flat surface. I turned my hand to inspect it, and realized that the thing was embossed on both sides with a capitol letter H.

H must stand for Hell. The food must have been made and stamped in Hell's kitchen. Then again, H could stand for Heaven. Or for the Hilton Group. Maybe the management of Eternity had been outsourced to a hotel chain. As I pondered the meaning of H, paying too little attention to the chaos around me, I was seized by outstretched hands and dragged out of the food trough. I hollered through a mouthful of biscuit and tried to scrabble up as many as possible in my fingers.

All around me people escaped from the food cavern, hunching protectively over their earnings, waddling, clutching biscuits to their abdomens, wheezing through the biscuits crammed in their mouths, squeezing biscuits in their arm pits, pinching them beneath their chins, hopping ridiculously with biscuits stuck between their filthy toes. I saw somebody collapse, his haul of biscuits spilling over the floor, spewing out of his mouth, while his eyes stood out and he choked silently. I was afraid he would die. I was naive enough to hesitate and watch him, wondering if I should stamp on his back to help him, when a biscuit shot out of his throat, hit the sewer muck on the floor, and made a tiny impact crater. He took a gigantic noisy breath, his eyes veined, the dread still in his face, and began to collect his treasure in a panic.

Clutching my own biscuit loot, I hurried away and found a dry place to sit by myself against the wall of a thinly populated cavern. Squatting in the shadows, I spat out the biscuits in my mouth, added them to the ones in my hands, and gloated over the satisfying pile of food on the floor beside me. I didn't intend to eat it right away. My stomach had shriveled from starvation and couldn't fit any more just then. Never mind. I could sit and rest, idly watch the crowd pass, reach out a hand when the mood took me and eat. . . .

But I didn't yet have the luxury. As I relaxed, my back against the wall, I began to detect the biscuits in my stomach taking on water. They were sucking the moisture out of my tissues and expanding.

A dreadful thirst came over me and all my gloating satisfaction disappeared. I didn't know whether to lie still, paralyzed by bloat, or to get up and hunt for water, but the thirst got the better of me and I staggered to my feet, my stomach distended and wobbling. I left my pile of biscuits behind and rushed back into the crowd.

There is no motivation like thirst. I was past collapse, but I stayed on my feet. My emaciated legs felt like dried sticks about to snap after all my recent exertion, but I could not stop fighting. I scratched my way through the crowd. I lost all kindness. I tore at people's hair and skin, I hit, I elbowed myself into gaps in the crowd, I screamed. The caves were filled with moving obstacles that I no longer recognized as people. They were bags of stuff with legs. I didn't care if I hurt those bags, if they would only get out of my way.

Miles through an incomprehensible tangle of caves and routes, I found water—a cluster of rusty pipes bristling out of a wall, dribbling. The crowd rioted in the space under the nozzles, fighting for territory, catching the rain in their mouths, licking the moisture off the wall, sucking up the semi-clean water that pooled on the floor. I plunged into the celebrating brawl and fought to the prime real estate directly under the pipes, where a beaded curtain of water fell over my face. Drinking splashes of that tepid, rusty water felt like life itself flowing into my stomach and dispersing into my brain. It was joy and absolution. It was anointment. I had become a member of the multitude in spirit, in emotion, in greed, and now finally in satisfaction.

CHAPTER 6

So I was inducted from microcosm to macrocosm. I began to realize that my old world, as complex as it had seemed, as multiplicative as the possibilities might have been between three people, was only a scale model of the macrocosm. I could not guess at the number of people crammed together. Every moment, new faces loomed at me in the dimness. I told myself that I had not so much lost two companions as gained a billion. I tried hard to feel the warmth of universal inclusion. From many, one. From strife, love. A tessellation. A motet of uncountable voices. Especially when I was sitting comfortably, my back to the stone wall, my legs stretched out, my stomach filled up with biscuits and water, I could watch the crowd magnanimously and grasp the unity. At least I thought I could. I tried. I pretended.

A never-ending labyrinth of caves.

An exponential branching of paths.

An infinite topology that could never be remembered, never retraced.

A biscuit economy.

Grace by rusty water.

The strong, deep, fundamental obsessions of the crowd: hunger, thirst, rage, joy, despair.

The honesty of anonymity.

The honest stench of piss and shit.

The exhibitionism of naked bodies and raw emotions.

The food stations were dotted here and there, separated from the water stations by miles of kinked paths. As a result, we were forced into a nomadic existence, always searching for one or the other, never remembering the paths we had just walked, never knowing where we were going. The geometry turned us into molecules in perpetual circulation.

Only determination could get to the food and the water, and whoever had the most frenzied determination won. The trick was that simple. Once I realized it, I had no difficulties. With exercise, my body hardened. I lost my gut. My stick legs thickened and strengthened. I felt alive, my skin glowed under the layer of black muck, and sometimes I poked at the bunched muscles on my arms and the sheath of my abdomen in amazement.

I was *good* at hell.

I was no longer like the people who crammed biscuits and lurched out of the food caverns temporarily insane with excitement. They were ineffective hunters. They never knew when the next meal might come because they lacked determination. When they could, they ate themselves fat, ate themselves sick, and then starved themselves flabby. Most of their biscuits were stolen from them anyway. For myself, I learned to take what I needed and then get away from the fight as quickly as I could.

I needed six and a half biscuits each time. No more. I chewed down four on the spot and left the other two and a half in my mouth to soften up for later. Then I went in search of water. Then I found a place to sleep.

I never stopped looking for Henry and Rose. Of all the people I encountered, all the faces I stared at in curiosity or hope, all the bodies I stumbled up against, none lifted me, none made me happy, none were as important to me as Henry and Rose, who were only faces in my mind now, remembrances. They were no better than anyone else, no more lovely than the thousand other people I saw every moment, no less filthy, but all the same they were *themselves*, they were special because I knew them, because I had spent enough time pressed up against them to absorb a little part of their odor and skin and blood and emotion, because they were after all my friends. I wanted *them*. I wanted, sometimes, to go back home. The more I searched, the less hope I had.

I couldn't even make a new friend. I would only lose the friend in the crowd, the next time I searched for a meal or a drink. The rules of the divine game resulted in a certain isolation of the soul.

THE DIVINE FARCE

The place was not entirely devoid of companionship, at least at its most biological. Especially near water stations, I noticed the conjugal instinct crawling out of the muck. Maybe we felt so euphoric after a good drink of water that our minds turned more hopefully toward each other. Or maybe a little extra liquid was necessary for the biology to work. Here and there I'd see couples braced against the walls, face to face, or face to back, their muddy feet planted sturdily apart in the sewage, their expressions intent, focused on the moment. I saw pigs heaving themselves sloppily onto the backs of pigs. I saw monkeys pinning each other by the fur and thrusting like mechanical drills. Prelude was strictly unnecessary. If I caught a woman's eye and she caught mine, if the look on her face posed the same question that I was asking, then we did what was in us to do. A moment later, breaking apart, we reluctantly lost each other in the neverending movement of the crowd.

I'd find a dry place to sleep at the edge of a cavern. Curling up on the floor, I'd feel paradoxically full in the stomach, empty in my heart, tired, alone, content, whole, hollow, broken and repaired, cheated and lucky, useless and essential to the cosmic pattern. On that ambivalent mood, as fascinating as a pillow, my mind would ease into sleep.

Then I'd wake up, put aside whatever doubts I had, and join the battle again.

CHAPTER 7

I was resting in the middle of a dead-end cavern, lying on my back, sucking on half a biscuit and looking up at the circles of light fifty feet above me. A woman was sitting a few feet away, her legs crossed, her back hunched, her elbows on her knees, her face caged in her long thin fingers. She looked like a tall woman. If she had unbent herself and stood up, she might have been taller than me. She was skeletally thin, only the contours of her face showing any lingering femininity, her hair long and clumped, her dry, scabbed lips parted slightly. The sole of her left foot, visible from my perspective, was shriveled and lined like the palm of an old person's hand. She was so still that she could have been dead, propped up on her elbows, brittle from rot, ready to disarticulate at a touch, except that her eyes roved.

Occasionally she blinked.

I sat up, took the half biscuit out of my mouth, and handed it to her. The act made no sense. From the point of view of pragmatism, it was a sin. I was wasting my hard earned food. From the point of view of kindness it was futile. I was embarrassed by the gesture, but I made it anyway. I didn't bother to speak—nobody spoke in that place. I squatted and held the biscuit out toward her, and her eyes swiveled down and looked at it.

At first she seemed too dead to respond. Her eyes drifted slowly up from the biscuit to my face and stared at nothing, as if I were emptiness. Then they moved back down to the biscuit. I was afraid she had exhausted her repertoire, but finally she took one of her hands from her face, her fingers leaving behind red vertical pressure-marks over her cheek and nose, and reached for the biscuit. She put the food in her mouth, caged her face in her fingers again, and resumed her torpor.

I waited, but she did nothing else. Her eyes moved glassily around the cave.

THE DIVINE FARCE

I felt ill, as if I had just done something grotesque. I didn't know why I felt such a strong self revulsion. Maybe I couldn't find anything else to blame. Not her—she was not at fault. Not the game—it was what it was. The blame was like a bird looking for somewhere to perch, and in my mind it decided to perch on me for no justifiable reason. It made me feel sick. I shouldn't have offered her food. I shouldn't have treated her on a whim. I shouldn't have crouched in front of her and taken so close a look at the emptiness in her face. I shouldn't have felt smug about my own strength and success. I began to stumble away from her, but before I could stand up and turn away she muttered, "I want more."

Nobody had spoken to me since Henry and Rose. I measured time in meals—and thousands of meals had passed without a sentence. Nobody spoke in this world. Nobody bothered, except to swear at each other, and I heard a lot of that. Now the woman in front of me had put three words together and I was frightened and didn't know how to respond.

"I . . . I'll bring you more," I mumbled. "Okay."

Her face was immobile behind the cage of her fingers. Her eyes wandered, staring at nothing, and I didn't know if she had heard me.

I backed away, anxious to get out of the cavern. I had no possible way to bring her any more food.

Even if I had superhuman memory, if I could find a food station and retrace the thousand odd turns of the path back to this particular cavern without a single error, if I had heroic strength and could fight through the crowd and stop it from carrying me in unwanted directions and losing me, even presuming the woman was still here to be found, even presuming I could find her in the gloom by bending down and checking each face until I recognized her out of the thousand hunched-over catatonic bodies littered across the enormous vault, I'd still fail, because I would not have enough food to make a difference. If I carried the biscuits in my hands, they would be stolen on the way. If I carried a decent supply in my cheeks, the bulge would give me away and I'd be attacked and robbed. At best I'd be able to give her two and a half biscuits carried discreetly in the back of my mouth. Even presuming two and a half biscuits were enough to feed her, they would do her no good without water, and I didn't know how to carry water.

CHAPTER 8

I was often robbed of my food, especially if I chewed too obviously. Once a man leaped on me, wrapped his arms and legs around my body and brought us both down in the muck on the floor. We rolled, his fingers clawing at my jaw, my hands spread out on his face while I pushed with all my strength to get him off. In the middle of the fight I opened my lips, my teeth still tightly clenched, and said in a muffled grunt, "Henry?"

The man was so startled that he paused in the fight, opened his eyes wide, and said, "What?"

"It's me, it's Sage."

"Who? What are you calling me?"

The fight was over. We sat back in the mud, eyeing each other and panting while I rubbed at my jaw.

He was about the right size and build,

thickly muscled, bald, his face folded into harsh lines.

"You think you know me?" he said, his dark eyes fixed on me curiously. His voice was filled with astonishment and a shy hope almost like a child's.

"Aren't you Henry? You and me and Rose, we were together..." He wasn't Henry. I could see it now.

He spread out his hands and shrugged, still breathing hard from the fight. He looked disappointed, his body sagging, his head sinking down.

"Do you still want a biscuit?" I asked, pulling one out of my mouth and handing it to him.

He took it and we sat side by side chewing.

"I haven't had a friend in a long time," he admitted.

After a while we got up and went separate ways.

CHAPTER 9

Is it enough to struggle in an endless cycle for the simple biological truths of food, water, sex, and sleep? I tried. I tried to be content. I tried not to feel nauseous about the failures of other people, to draw my satisfaction from the strength of my own muscles and bones. Success is selfish. I tried to relegate my friends to an idle dream. I pretended to a certain nonchalance, as if I didn't need anyone and was quite well off on my own, but at the same time I kept an eye out ceaselessly for Henry and Rose. Sometimes my pretense worked for me, but sometimes my brain acted up and wanted a different answer. When the frustration came over me, I'd take a break from the perpetual fight, sit down, lean back against a wall, and wonder what else, what else is in the world? What else is worth doing? I thought the question was rhetorical, or at least metaphorical, until a literal answer came to me as I was watching a cloud of bats.

I had finished eating and was resting, my back propped up against a pile of broken stones and pebbles banked against the wall, my hands folded over my stomach. The bats were about the size of my palm and moved in starts and flitters, abruptly changing direction, weaving among each other without collision as if performing a practiced choreography. The light tinged their wings, giving them a flickering appearance, sometimes silver, sometimes brown, sometimes fading into shadow. When they flew high, near the lights on the ceiling, they stood out small and clear, and when they dropped down toward the crowd they dissolved into a half-guessed movement in the gloom. A thin crowd of a few hundred people sifted through the cavern, but I was the only one looking up at the bats.

They were hunting flies. The flies lived on our refuse, arguably putting us at the bottom of the food chain, the flies next, and the bats at the top. They were graceful at any rate, and we were not.

The bats had a strange and exhilarating effect on me. They made me feel connected to the light bulbs dotted across the ceiling. It was as if their flight carried threads of imagination up and down that stitched me to a mystery.

As I was watching, lying back against the pile of stony rubble, I saw a single bat flitter up and disappear. I waited for it to turn again and catch the light, but it hadn't disappeared in the usual method of maneuver or camouflage. It was simply gone. It had flown up and turned into nothing. The realization grew on me slowly—that animal had flown through a light and left the cavern.

Suddenly my perception clicked and I realized that the lights were holes riddling the black rock. They were so high and dim that I hadn't seen them properly. They weren't spheres hanging from the underside of the rock—they were apertures, and the light was shining down from a space above the cavern.

I scrambled to my feet, staring up at the lights, moving my head side to side. Maybe my vision had played a trick. I reached out and touched someone's shoulder as he was passing. "Did you know there's a space up there?"

He turned and looked at me out of a shower of hair.

"Above the ceiling," I said, pointing.

He inspected my finger as if I was talking about it instead of the ceiling.

"I just saw a bat fly through a light and escape."

His eyes moved from my finger to my face. He looked carefully all around my lips, and I knew what he was doing. He was looking for crumbs or any reflectance of grease that might indicate a biscuit hidden in my mouth. He was deciding whether or not to rob me. With a grunt, he turned and continued on his way.

I was so taken by the idea of a space above the ceiling that I walked around the cavern to look from different perspectives. The floor was uneven. I stood on the high corner, several feet above the rest of the floor, staring up, my face screwed up, my upper lip pulled back from my teeth in concentration. Although I watched the bats carefully, I didn't see any more of them disappear.

The possibility of an extra space made me happy. The accommodations of hell, presuming it was hell, were enormous, possibly infinite, but had a way of closing in around the soul. Stench and steam and motion and ego and frustration, excreted by the crowd, oozed into the enormous space. No matter how large the cavern, that cloudy gelatin filled it up and squeezed me. The thought of extra space above the ceiling made me feel as though the world had suddenly expanded and the substance within it was therefore that much more rarefied and pleasanter to breathe.

CHAPTER 10

Reach as high as you can. Ascend to heaven. Rise to the challenge. Stretch to the sky. Elevate your mind. Seek knowledge at the summit. Attain the pinnacle of joy, the peak of success, the spire of aspire, the loft of lofty.

I aspired to look into those holes.

Exotic fancies went through my mind. I could climb a giraffe and stand on its head, if it let me, but I would gain only about twenty feet. I could cling to the back of an orangutan. I had seen them scaling up to the water pipes, but I couldn't imagine one climbing fifty feet up the wall, especially with a person on its back.

I could hang to the feet of a thousand bats.

More pragmatically, I could pick up a stone and throw it at one of those lights. It wouldn't bring me any closer to the ceiling, but if the rock passed through and never came back down, it would prove for certain that the lights were openings into another place.

I picked up a pebble and threw it as hard as I could with a gasp of effort. It shrank away from me, and the bats swarmed it as if it were a bug. They turned away as it arced back down toward the floor, and they ignored the second pebble that I threw.

The best stones fit nicely in my palm with a comfortable heft. I could hit the ceiling with them. As to my aim being good enough to hit one of the lights—I left that to luck.

My stones fell back, exploding on the floor, landing with a splash in sewage, hitting people in the crowd. I saw someone cringing and running. I was sorry to damage her and tried to aim so that the stones would rattle harmlessly down the wall instead of dropping into the middle of the room.

Finally one of my stones flew straight toward a light, passed into the illuminated circle, and disappeared like an act of divine intervention.

THE DIVINE FARCE

I stared up at that light for a long time, my neck kinked. Something from my hand had gone up and left the cavern. I had sent an emissary outside the world. My elation was so immense that I did not know how to express it. Instead of laughing and calling out to the apathetic crowd that sifted around me, I stood perfectly still, staring at the ceiling, scowling with concentration, my fists clenched.

Now my imagination began to soar. If I had a rope, I could tie a rock to the end of it and throw the rock. Maybe I could get the rock wedged up inside the ceiling firmly enough that the rope would hold my weight. Or maybe the rock would enter one hole and fall out another one, giving me a double-stranded ladder to the ceiling. If I could climb to the ceiling, I'd be able to look through one of the holes and see outside the world. I could try—if I had a rope.

The solution was obvious. My feet were perpetually tangled in it. The floors of every cavern were strewn with a wrack of sewage and hair. We were all naked in a world

filled with perfectly serviceable thread. Why
didn't we make shoes for ourselves? Why
didn't we make sacks to carry our biscuits instead of cramming them in our mouths and
screwing them in our colons? Why didn't we
make strings to pay out behind us and track
our way through the labyrinth? Why didn't
companions and lovers rope themselves together to avoid separation in the crowd?
The strangeness of the place began to dawn
on me. We were so driven by hunger and
thirst, and so isolated from each other by
the constant mixing of the crowd, and so
numbed by the repetition of caverns and
food troughs and rusty water pipes and perpetual battle, and so gratified at each orgiastic meal, that we had lost all our capacity
for imagination. For *vision*.

If death hands you rancid shit strewn with
human hair, make an escape ladder. Is that
a variant of the adage? I became an enthu-
siast. I set about twisting a rope for myself,
sitting cross-legged on the floor and scraping up a handful of sludge. Kneading and
pulling, my fingers black and the vapors

exploding in my face, I extracted hair and began to twist it into a thread. Some of the hairs were too short and curled, or split and brittle, and did me no good. I knotted the long scalp-strands together meticulously in square hitches, end to end, then braided them, my head bent down in the gloom, until I had a length of rope as thick as my finger, as long as my arm, glittering with yellow and platinum and brunette. I was surprised at the ease of the task. When I tried to stand up, however, I realized how long I must have been working. My knees hurt and my stomach felt pinched from hunger.

No matter. I had time. A hundred feet of rope was easy. I was inspired. I had a goal to sustain me and no end to the raw thread. I took breaks to eat, drink, and sleep, and worked in between. Nobody interrupted. Nobody cared.

"I'm making a rope," I said to a man who was sitting next to me in one cavern. We were on a dry part of the floor at the edge. He was leaning back against the wall, his chin down, his arms folded high across his chest. "I'll use it to climb out," I said. "What do you think?" I held up part of the rope and yanked on it to demonstrate its strength. His eyes slid toward me for a moment without expression, then closed.

As the rope grew, I began to wrap it around my waist to carry it with me. The weave was so dense that it weighed me down, but the rope was useful armor against claws and elbows. I could slam my way through the battle and get anywhere I wanted. Obtaining food and water became so easy that it was no longer a challenge. I did it as quickly as possible, and then returned to the more important endeavor.

Once, in a euphoric crowd that had just quenched its thirst at a water station, I was grabbed from behind by the dangling tail of my rope. I had unintentionally outfitted myself with a handle. The woman hauled me closer playfully, but I couldn't reciprocate. Unlike every other body in the crush, I was wearing clothes. I didn't want to risk losing my rope by unwrapping it and putting it aside. I smiled apologetically, shrugged, and declined. But under my smile I wondered why she was interested in the usual instead of in the rope. Nobody, absolutely nobody seemed to understand the cosmic importance of my discovery.

CHAPTER 11

When I thought I had enough rope, I sought out a dead-end cavern. I wanted a place where I could concentrate and not worry about the crowd surging around me. Finding a vast silent room littered with human derelicts, I lumbered to a bare patch near the center of the floor and began to unload.

I had one hundred feet of rope—soft, flexible and as thick as my wrist—wrapped around me from the hips to the armpits, coiled in layers. I could hardly breathe in that jacket. Underneath it, I had one hundred feet of string. Under the string, against my skin, I had a hoard of biscuits that I had slipped in bit by bit, and also a collection of useful rocks. I unwound myself, coiled the rope neatly on the floor, and hid the biscuits in a pile inside the coil. The stash of

MICHAEL S. A. GRAZIANO

food was meant to keep me while I concentrated on my experiment.

I selected a rock about the size of my fist and tied the end of the string around it. I intended to start with the string, because the thicker rope was too heavy to throw any distance. To cast the rock at the ceiling, I dangled it on a length of string about as long as my forearm, swung it in a whistling circle, and then released it, and it arced upward, the string trailing behind. My first cast flew at the wrong angle and crashed in the darkness somewhere else in the room. I retrieved it, following the string through the silent, hunched graveyard of people. The second cast was hardly better. As I continued to practice, I hit myself on the shin a few times swinging the rock, and clipped my ear, but I learned how to throw more or less straight up at the ceiling.

The rock was a hazard on the way down. The people around me muttered and shifted and looked about uneasily, roused out of their torpor. Luckily the rock missed them, but the string fell in a tangle on their heads.

THE DIVINE FARCE

As I unwound it from one man's bushy gray hair, he found the energy to jump up and scream in my face, his eyes enormous in his skull, his body shriveled like sticks. He didn't say anything. He only screamed.

"I'm trying to escape," I told him reasonably. "If I can escape, you can come too."

He lurched into the shadows. The others followed him. They glared at me and moved away crabwise, receding in a circle until the center of the floor was empty. I was alone. In the darkness I could hear them grumbling, coughing, resettling on the floor at a safe distance.

I worked by myself, casting the stone, running and flinching as it came back down at me, gathering up the string, casting it again.

The first time the stone flew up into a circle of light and lodged above me, I did not have the heart to pull on my cord. I held the end of it, looking up at its graceful curve. I was connected to the goal and I felt some measure of awe. I was certain the others would finally recognize the beauty of the endeavor, but when I stared around at the shadowy, distant audience, nobody stirred. They were absorbed in their own inner methods of escape.

Cringing, I pulled gently on the string, pulled a little harder, and the stone re-appeared and fell back down at me. The cast was no good.

I didn't feel determined. I certainly did not feel energetic. My enthusiasm had disappeared in exhaustion. I simply couldn't think of anything else to do. The routine of the caverns? Fighting, eating, drinking, fucking, wishing, pissing, shitting, sleeping, fighting, eating? The dense loneliness of it suddenly appalled me. I dreaded returning to it, and so I swung my rock on a theory and an unlikely chance, released it, let it fly toward the ceiling, retrieved it, and swung it again. At least I had found something different to do.

Even though the string was as soft as a braid, the friction of it slipping rapidly through my fingers, cast after cast, began to wear a stripe through my skin.

The Divine Farce

One cast was exceptionally good. I had learned to use minimal movement, saving my energy and letting inertia and the swing of the rope do the work for me. I watched the stone shoot up and pass easily into the light. Then gently I pulled on the string. The stone fell back out of the same hole and dropped down.

Again I had a good cast. The stone had good momentum when it disappeared. I thought I could hear it clattering somewhere above the ceiling. When I tugged on the string, pulling gently, the stone appeared in a neighboring hole, about a yard away from the one it had first gone in, bobbing and dangling just below the ceiling. I was so shocked by the fact of success that I almost pulled too hard and ruined the moment. Listen, I said to myself. Whoever you are. Brother Brian Blue, if that is still who you are. Now is the time to be careful. You're much too tired for cleverness.

Slowly I let out the string, paying it into one hole while the rock lowered out of the neighboring hole, until it came down and rested on the ground at my feet. The string was now looped through the ceiling.

The string, of course, was much too light to hold my weight. I took its free end and tied it to my thick length of rope. The hitch had to be absolutely secure. When I was confident, I pulled on the opposite end of the string, raising my heavy rope toward the ceiling, the coils unwinding on the ground next to me. The rope passed easily into the hole in the ceiling and then reappeared, snaking out of the neighboring hole. With a growing feeling of exaltation, I pulled until the heavy rope was looped entirely through the ceiling, both ends hanging in front of me.

I tied a knot at one end of my rope. I judged the holes in the ceiling to be about five inches across, and to err on the side of prudence I tied a giant, dense, tangle of a knot about the size of a human head. Hauling on the other end of the rope, I raised my knot in the air until it reached the ceiling and jammed against the hole. I could not pull the rope any tighter. It was fixed in place. I swung on it and it easily supported my weight. My route to the ceiling was complete.

As I stared up at the ceiling, someone crept toward me across the floor. I heard the noise, looked down, and saw a man snatch up my hoard of biscuits. He glanced up at me with a mixture of derision and triumph. Then he scurried into the shadows, his hands clutched to his boney chest.

He hadn't cared about the rope. He only wanted the food.

I wasn't angry about the robbery itself—I had too much experience with biscuit economics to be surprised—but I was dismayed by the universal contempt for my ladder. Was I insane? I believed I had something astounding—a rope beside me that ascended straight to the ceiling. I had *a way out*. Was I wrong? Was I blind to the simple truths that everyone else found self-evident?

Instead of swarming up the rope and exploring the ceiling, I sat on the floor with my face in my hands and doubted myself. But I didn't know if the queasy feeling in my stomach was truly self-doubt or just hunger.

I could not get around one practical truth. If I gave up the experiment and plunged back into circulation, looking for food and water, surviving as I had learned to do, I would never find my rope ladder again. My work and bruises and bloody hands and mental anguish would be wasted. With that thought, and a grim set to my mouth, I stood up and began to climb, pinching the rope between my knees to steady myself, wincing and gasping at the pain in my skinned hands.

The light grew and the air smelled cleaner. The steam and stench and heat seemed to fall away toward the floor. My eyes were fixed above me on the round lights, and as I inched closer I could see clearly that they were holes in a slab. But even when I was directly under the ceiling, and could reach up with one hand and touch it, and see that it was black painted concrete with a pebbly texture, I still could not quite see what was above it. I could not get a good look through the holes.

To touch the ceiling I had to grip the rope

hard with one hand and let go with the other. I groped into a hole and found that the ceiling was only a few inches thick. The concrete must have been reinforced with steel beams, otherwise the expanse would never stay up. As I was planning in my mind how to break through, I noticed an irony in attending to the practical and mechanical in the presence of mystery. (Who riveted the beams and poured the concrete? Had they worn yellow hard hats?) With my hand spread out on the bumpy surface, I felt as if I were touching the belly of a pregnant woman. A new possibility lay hidden here. But I didn't know which side was inside and which was out. Was I the obstetrician or the baby?

When I climbed down to find a hammering stone, the stink and heat rose around me like a wet sludgy cloth leaking fluid into my nose and mouth. Scrambling on the ground on my hands and knees, trying not to breathe, I found a good hammer. It had a thin part sticking out that I could hold between my teeth while my hands were occupied in climbing.

The challenge of hammering at the ceiling was to hang one-handed from the rope, my grip aching, my fingers turning white, and in a frenzied moment strike as accurately as I could at the concrete, knock off a pebble or a few grains of matrix, transfer the hammer back to my mouth, and seize the rope again with both hands before I lost my grip; then rest a moment; then take another one-handed swipe at the concrete. When I mis-struck I skinned my knuckles, but I managed to keep hold of the hammer. With practice I discovered a fast, sharp snap of the wrist that chipped the concrete particularly well. When I couldn't hang to the rope any longer, even two-handed, and the cords in my wrists felt like they would rip from their points of attachment on the bone, I put the hammer between my teeth, shinned down the rope and stood on the floor, resting, rubbing my wrists, struggling to breathe the thick air, looking up at the ceiling. I was surprised at the progress. The ceiling light that I was working on was no longer a perfect circle. It was a misshapen blob of light. I had knocked it twice as large already.

By now I was beginning to crave water. I was afraid I might collapse or lose control and run out of the cavern in insanity before finishing the job. I wanted at least to knap the hole wide enough to get my head up and look around. Each time that I climbed up and hammered at the ceiling, chips flew in my eyes, black dust went down my lungs, and my mouth was so dry from thirst that I could not spit out the grains of debris. But the concrete was not as difficult to break apart as I expected. Perhaps it had absorbed too much of the moist funk of the underworld. By my seventh trip to the top of the rope, I had an aperture large enough to crawl through.

I probably should have rested before the final push, but I was impatient. I reached into the hole and blindly put my stone hammer on the flat surface above me. Then I scrabbled with my fingers to find a grip. Dragging myself up, one hand clinging to the rope, the other clawed onto the dusty, slippery, crumbling edge of concrete, my arms trembling with the effort, my feet kicking, I dangled between one world and the next. I should have smoothed the edge. Concrete points gouged my skin as I slid over the lip. Finally I pulled up enough of my body to lie on my stomach, my legs hanging down through the hole I had carved, my breath like broken stone in my throat, my energy spent, my sight faded and jostled by black spots, a trickle of urine escaping from me and falling back down into the dimness of the cavern below. I was so tired that I no longer had control over any muscle in my body.

CHAPTER 12

I was on a silent, geometrically perfect plane of concrete, unpainted, gray, unending. It was covered in a thin gritty dust, like moon dust, evenly spread and undisturbed except near me where I could see streaks in the shape of my own clawed fingers. I was alone. I saw no sign that anyone had ever been here since it was made.

The concrete was perforated with holes, randomly sprinkled but more or less evenly distributed, blending in the distance into the even gray. From below they had looked like lights; from above they looked like black spots. Steam rose out of the holes and dissipated in the cooler air.

Here and there a metal lamp stood up. Each lamp was made of aluminum pipes—a tripod base, a tall central pole, and a bulb at the top, an industrial bulb with a slightly yellowed tint, angled and shining down from a height of about ten feet. The electrical cord from each lamp stretched upward from the bulb, glittering orange in the light, disappearing into a darkness overhead. I did not see any ceiling above me. Only a gigantic, sterile emptiness. A nothingness. Every sound I made had a crisp, precise quality, spreading into the nothingness without any possibility of resonance.

The place was so austere that for the first time my nakedness made me uneasy. This space above the ceiling was obviously not built for habitation and I was not meant to be here. I stood up in the light—tall, skinny, blotched a bit around the legs and arms from recent bruises, my abdomen moving in and out in slightly too rapid breaths, my penis shriveling up in anxiety, my feet too large in their caked shoes of fecal muck. The strange chessboard expanded around me and confused my eyes. The regularity of it gave me vertigo. Every time I moved my head I felt as if the floor had taken a wobble.

THE DIVINE FARCE

I was afraid that if I walked away from my exit hole across the apparently infinite floor I might never find my way back again. But when I took a few steps, barefoot and silent over the concrete slab, I made a trail of footprints in the dust. I could always retrace the footprints.

I prowled naked through the bright blankness.

I saw a shadow crouching ahead. Given the fantastical range of animals in the caverns below, I thought of a rhinoceros, or a dead whale, but whatever it was, it did not move. I approached slowly. Finally I was close enough to make out a square metal tank resting on the concrete floor. It was about the height of my shoulder and was made of gray, galvanized steel. Black letters stenciled on the side read: Water Station 66453A. It was open at the top, and looking in over the side I saw that it was half filled with clean water. The tank was replenished by a copper pipe that came straight down from the darkness above. I could not see the origin of the pipe—it disappeared in the upper emptiness. A small hole at the bottom of the tank, visible under the surface, presumably carried the water into the caverns below.

I was so thirsty that I scrambled over the side of the tank and fell into the water. Nobody stopped me. I had no competition, no crowd, no fight, no screaming, no one pulling me away by the hair. I did not need to tilt my head back to catch the sparse droplets of a rusty rain. Kneeling on the metal bottom, I put my mouth to the surface and sucked up as much as I wanted. It filled my stomach—and when I closed my eyes and concentrated, I thought I could feel the water diffusing into my tissues, reconstituting them. The water was cool, soothing to my joints and the scrapes on my hands, and seemed to draw the pains and bruises out of my skin and dissolve them away.

I took a bath. I scratched the mud off myself with my fingernails and indulged in the strange, lovely sensation of cleanliness. Even my black sewage shoes and socks disappeared. I lifted up a foot to see, and it looked new and pale with branching veins under the skin. I washed the tack and mud and fossilized pear nectar from my hair. The galvanized sides of the tank boomed every time I hit them, and I began to hammer on them with my fists and bellow a song. The din was outrageous and exhilarating, spreading around me into emptiness.

When the water had turned a thick yellow-brown, I clambered out and stood wet on the concrete floor, a puddle spreading around my feet and dripping down the nearest hole. It occurred to me a little late that I had dirtied the drinking water for the people below. Crouching, I put my face to the hole and peered into the dimness. The smell was putrid. The shadows fifty feet below me changed and mingled, but in a moment my eyes adjusted and I figured out what I was seeing. As I expected, it was a water station—a rabble of creatures fighting for space under the drizzle. They did not seem to mind that the water had turned muddy. I used to be down among them. I used to be a part of that mob, and now I was free.

I wandered around the utility space in a dream, in a daze at the beauty of solitude and open space, at the tactile beauty of a clean skin, leaving wet footprints, spying down on the crowd here and there. Where the crowd was dense, steam rose up out of the holes. Sometimes flies came up, but mainly they stayed below with the refuse. If bats flittered up, they were so rare that I didn't see any. I was alone. No people screaming in my face or clawing past me or robbing me. No more muck. Abundant food stations and water stations and great round vats of pear nectar and tomato juice and apple juice and banana puree. I could take anything I wanted. I could pick up a handful of the hard round biscuits, carry them, soak them in a vat of juice to soften them, and eat them at my leisure. I could sleep wherever I wanted and nobody stepped on me.

But the sterility of the space did begin to worry me.

As I drifted about the emptiness, leaving an increasingly Byzantine trail of footsteps behind me, I tried to pinpoint exactly what made the place so disturbing. Partly it offered me no insight. I had escaped the public halls and crawled into the machine penthouse, a utility space, a place for maintenance and builders, and examined the machinery itself, looked at it and touched it, jumped in it and banged on it, and after all had learned nothing about the purpose. Nobody seemed to have made the place. Nobody seemed to maintain it. It was here—that was all I could say definitively. It was here and it was extremely large. It was what it was. It had a logic that was utilitarian.

The solitude also nagged at me. In the crowd below, the density of people had squeezed me into anonymity. Here I experienced a bone-cold isolation that put a new perspective on mere anonymity. Sometimes I lay on the floor on my stomach, my face to one of the holes, and stared down at the crush of people and animals. The light below was so dim that I could not see faces clearly. Only motion, noise, smell, shadows. Was that dreadful place down there so bad?

Is it possible to be alone when other people are pressed against you skin to skin?

I began to think that people must shed a chemical, like an insect pheromone, something in the sweat, in the oil on the skin, in the smell aerosolized by armpit hair and pubic hair, something that swaps around and spreads and gets up people's nostrils and in their pores, and comforts the brain, the chemical essence of companionship, so that even if you snarl at those people around you, or ignore them, or fight them to the food and the water, and never say a diplomatic word to them, still you feel the mass of human comfort sustaining you. When I looked down at that crowd and smelled that horrible rotting odor, I felt I was catching just enough of the airborne drug to rouse my craving for it, not enough to give me the satisfaction of a proper fix. I didn't know whether I wanted to go back down into that mess or stay above it. For the death of me, I couldn't tell whether the place was intended to be heaven or hell. To the extent that heaven above is isolation, it seems to be hell. To the extent that hell below is a crowd, it apparently is heaven. Maybe we are condemned to an endless nagging sense of discomfort balanced against comfort, satisfaction against the itch to escape. But having escaped as far as I had, I didn't know where else to go.

So I drifted. I slept and ate. I wandered across the endless blankness and asked, what should I do now? Should I go back? Should I stay?

I retraced my steps to the entrance hole, not to climb back down, but to retrieve my hammering rock and my rope. I carried them with me after that. I could climb down again if the urge ever overcame me, and it was a comfort to know I had the option.

Once, when I was lying on the floor taking a nap, I noticed that I was directly over a dead-end cavern. I could see no motion below me, only the half-guessed shadows of people dotting the floor. Starving people who had given up the fight. The place was silent. None of the usual noise of the crowd rose up out of the holes at me. On a sudden thought, the memory of a promise, I jumped up and walked to the nearest food tank. It was not far away. Down below it would have been difficult to find through a branching tangle of paths, but up above I could see it clearly and made a straight line to it. I gathered an armful of biscuits, hundreds of them, hugging them to my stomach, and then walked back, retracing my footsteps in the dust. I dumped the biscuits down the holes, kicked down the strays, and lay on my stomach to watch. I thought I could hear the echoing chatter of the biscuits hitting the floor. Then I began to see a commotion like bugs crawling in the shadows. People were moving. They stirred, reached out, picked up the food, and noises came up to me—the sound of fighting.

I played God. Why not? I thought I was stepping into a vacancy. I took to shedding food, strewing it over the caverns. It was a way to feel connected to the warmth. I dropped food over a water station, mucking with the logic that drove the crowds in circulation. I soaked biscuits until they swelled up and turned into watery mush, priceless meals, and dropped them here and there as if dispensing grace. From my hand came plenty. I could not distinguish individual faces in the shadows, but I could imagine the eagerness and the orgiastic joy.

Everywhere I wandered I saw caverns spreading beneath me, food stations, water stations, mazes crushed with people, an unending pageant of faceless shadows, an infinity that I could only dimly understand and that I could not possibly feed or help or move or alter or harm in any substantial way. My masquerade as a god felt more and more ridiculous.

Who made this place? Who runs it? Does it have a purpose? For myself, I seemed to have a repertoire, if not a purpose, and my repertoire was limited. I was, apparently, a wanderer. Was that the right word? I bashed my way out of one place and into another. I had fallen out of a chrysalis, fought through concrete and crowds, scaled heights, and achieved—what exactly? Ambiguity. Gains and losses in uneasy balance. A naked drift farther away and farther out from the truth of my original home. I never seemed to reach a goal. Maybe the exploration itself was a purpose. I couldn't think of any other. Just like the purpose of a hammer is to hit things, I had no other way to relate to the substance around me except to do what was in me to do. That was not a satisfying answer, but it was all I could think of.

And I had a lot of time to think, lying on my back with a tangle of rope as a pillow, my hands crossed over my chest, my eyes on the pure darkness above me, looking at the pipes and wires that came down from the void like the strings of marionettes dangling over a stage.

The more grandiose I let my thoughts become, the less the world made sense. The more focused my thoughts became on the specific, on the mundane, on the pragmatic, the more of the mystery I understood. That in itself was a paradox worth considering.

The purpose of the strange, cold, utilitarian logic of the world? I didn't know. But the cuts on my feet, finally beginning to heal? Little white scars that I could feel with a gentle distinctness against the pads of my fingers? Not only did I understand them, but they seemed to throw a glow of meaning around me. If walking was a joy instead of a wincing shuffle, then surely the world made that much more sense?

I invented plans, delicious fantasies. I imagined climbing down, finding a companion, and convincing her to follow me to the space above the world. I knew from experience how difficult it was to convince anyone of anything, but difficult was not the same as impossible. The sensible plan was to find a water station. People opened up to each other in the euphoria of drinking. I'd knock a hole in the ceiling and hang my rope, then climb down and wait, and watch, and talk to people, and take my time, and try to find someone with enough imagination to climb back up with me. Someone friendly, someone kind, someone with a sense of wonder, someone worthy of the fantasy. I constructed her in my mind.

And yet my thoughts came back and back

to Henry and Rose. They troubled me. I began to unpack in my memory the luminous sounds of their voices in resonance. The architecture of their faces. The exact curvature of Rose's eyebrows, one slightly different from the other. The square set to Henry's jaw. The texture of our three-way intimacy. After all the slow ages of knowing them in darkness I had seen them in the light only briefly, but I still remembered what they looked like. I remembered how surprised I was by the waddling inelegance of their bodies. So be it. Mine was no better. And I could remember especially the look on Henry's face when the crowd separated us. It was the last I ever saw of him, that agony as if, at the moment the crowd had pulled us apart, the strands connecting my heart to his had physically ripped out his insides.

The old reality, our old world, black and blazing with imagined color, cramped and psychologically immense, was only a remembered thing, but it still had more hold on me than any fantasy I could think up. In my bones, in my gut, in my hands, in my cut-up feet, in every part of my body I wanted to find my Henry and my Rose. The feeling became like acid running through my veins, until I said to myself, let it be a disaster. Let it be a long search. Let them come up here, if I ever do find them, and fight with me. Let them bring all their quirks and annoyances that I know very well. Ten thousand other people are probably better suited to me and deserve the luxury above the muck, but it doesn't matter. My friends have precedence.

So I conceived of a new purpose. Or maybe it was always the purpose, part of the same arc of wandering. If I could learn the biscuit game, and outfight the competition, and overcome the discouraging indifference of the crowd, and weave ropes out of sewage, and thread a rock through a hole fifty feet above me, and chip through concrete, and pull myself up bloody and exhausted and successful, if I could do all those difficult and imaginative—that is to say crazy—things, then couldn't I use this forbidding place above the world to search for my friends? What better platform could I find? It seemed made for the purpose. There was that word again—purpose.

"Henry, Rose!" I called down into the caverns. "I can rescue you! Are you there?"

Are you there?

Now I am the strange mad creature of the ceiling. Obsessed and content with that obsession. To have a purpose is in itself an arrival.

Pieces of concrete fall, sprinkle the floor, splash in the sewage, a hole opens up, a voice flares down, a light bulb shines, the cavern is illuminated, the light turns and flickers around the vault, picks out the corners, falls on upturned faces, hovers, spins, pauses again, then withdraws. Cavern after cavern, searching an endless tide. I do not intend to give up. I will find you. In the mathematics of infinite hope against infinite numbers, my success is inevitable. I've already seen six pseudo-Roses and three ersatz-Henrys. I knew they weren't you—I had to look closely, but I figured it out. When I do find you, the real you, one at a time or maybe both together, I'll come swinging down on a rope, beating my chest, and then you will be amazed. Then we will be together again, almost like it was before, only better.

THE AUTHOR

Drawing by Wurge

Michael S. A. Graziano, Ph.D., is a professor of psychology at Princeton University. When not doing research Michael spends his time writing fiction and composing music. He lives in Princeton, N.J., with his family.

ABOUT THE TYPE

This book was set in ITC New Baskerville, a typeface based on the types of John Baskerville (1706-1775), an accomplished printer from Birmingham, England. The excellent quality of his printing influenced such famous printers as Didot in France and Bodoni in Italy. Baskerville produced a masterpiece folio Bible for Cambridge University, and today, his types are considered to be fine representations of eighteenth century rationalism and neoclassicism. This ITC New Baskerville was designed by Matthew Carter and John Quaranda in 1978.

Designed by John Taylor-Convery
Composed at JTC Imagineering, Santa Maria, CA